CHILLERS

The Blob

TESSA POTTER

Illustrated by
PETER COTTRILL

CHILLERS

The Blob Tessa Potter and Peter Cottrill
Clive and the Missing Finger Sarah Garland
The Day Matt Sold Great-grandma Eleanor Allen and Jane Cope
The Dinner Lady Tessa Potter and Karen Donelly
Ghost from the Sea Eleanor Allen and Leanne Franson
Hide and Shriek! Paul Dowling
Jimmy Woods and the Big Bad Wolf Mick Gowar and Barry Wilkinson
Madam Sizzers Sarah Garland
The Real Porky Philips Mark Haddon
Sarah Scarer Sally Christie and Claudio Muñoz
Spooked Philip Wooderson and Jane Cope
Wilf and the Black Hole Hiawyn Oram and Dee Shulman

PUFFIN BOOKS

Published by the Penguin Group
Penguin Books Ltd, 27 Wrights Lane, London W8 5TZ, England
Penguin Books USA Inc., 375 Hudson Street, New York, New York 10014, USA
Penguin Books Australia Ltd, Ringwood, Victoria, Australia
Penguin Books Canada Ltd, 10 Alcorn Avenue, Toronto, Ontario, Canada M4V 3B2
Penguin Books (NZ) Ltd, 182–190 Wairau Road, Auckland 10, New Zealand

Penguin Books Ltd, Registered Offices: Harmondsworth, Middlesex, England

First published by A&C Black (Publishers) Ltd 1994
Published in Puffin Books 1996
3 5 7 9 10 8 6 4 2

Chapter One

The first blob appeared on Graham's book after second break. It was a rusty red colour. It looked wet and shiny but felt dry when you touched it.

Graham put his hand up.
"Miss, Miss."
"What is it Graham?"

Somebody's dropped something on my maths book

(Miss Merryman was on supply. Our real teacher Mrs North had flu. In fact nearly the whole school had flu. There were only twelve children left in our class. Even Miss Bell the Headteacher was away.)

"Let me see. Are you sure you haven't done this, Graham?"
"No, Miss. I haven't touched it. It was alright a minute ago."

I put up my hand. Graham was my best friend and I sat next to him.
"Honestly, he hasn't done it Miss. I've been right next to him all the time."
"Alright, thank you Jack," said Miss Merryman.

She held up the book so everybody could see it. There was quite a large red blob on it, about four centimetres across.

Has anybody done THIS to Graham's book?

Silence.

5

"Has anyone got any idea what this blob can be?"

The ideas came thick and fast.

Louise put up her hand.
"I think it's blood, Miss."
"Right, thank you everybody," said Miss Merryman, "that will be enough ideas for now."

She rubbed at the blob very carefully with her finger, half expecting it to come off.

Don't be silly, gravy's brown That's enough Tom.

She looked down at Graham again.
"Are you sure you don't know anything about this?"
"No, Miss!"
"You'd better try and get it off. The rest of you get on, please."

Graham rubbed his book so hard he made a hole in the cover. I could see he was fed up. He was sure Miss Merryman didn't believe him. After all, it was the kind of thing he might have done.

Chapter Two

It was very wet and windy at lunch-time.
Everyone stood around in little groups
trying to keep warm.

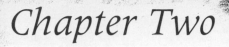

I kept thinking
about the blob.
What was it? Who'd
done it and when?

We'd all just got back
into class when Emma
suddenly screamed,

AAHHH

Everyone charged out of their seats to
look, but Miss Merryman sent us all back.

"This is ridiculous," she said. "Someone
must be responsible. Who has done this
to Emma's book?"

No-one said anything.

I put up my hand.
"What is it, Jack?"
"None of us could have done it, Miss. We
were all out at lunch-time. Someone else
must have come in."
"Well," sighed Miss Merryman, "I'd
better lock the classroom door in future."

10

We had quite a good first lesson. Miss Merryman called it "an excellent creative session". She was very pleased with us. We all had to write a short story in pairs called "The Blob" and illustrate it.

Most of the stories seemed to be science fiction.

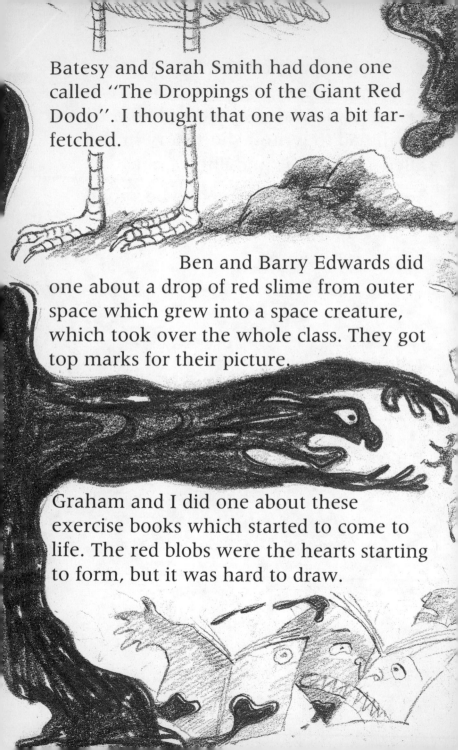

Batesy and Sarah Smith had done one called "The Droppings of the Giant Red Dodo". I thought that one was a bit far-fetched.

Ben and Barry Edwards did one about a drop of red slime from outer space which grew into a space creature, which took over the whole class. They got top marks for their picture.

Graham and I did one about these exercise books which started to come to life. The red blobs were the hearts starting to form, but it was hard to draw.

Tom Dent and Louise did a really gruesome one about a dead body in the upstairs classroom which kept dripping blood through the ceiling. Miss Merryman wasn't so keen on that one.

Then the bell went for break. Miss Merryman put our stories and pictures up on the wall and then locked the door and went to have her tea.

13

Miss Merryman was late getting back from break and because the door was locked we had to wait outside in the corridor. We all got told off by Mr Brown for making too much noise. (Mr Brown was acting as Deputy while Miss Bell was away, taking us for R.E. and extra reading and assembly. He'd only been here for two days. He was very tall and quiet and looked grim all the time. We didn't like him much.)

There was a lot of pushing and shoving
because everyone was trying to look
through the door to see if anything else
had happened. Batesy had got squashed
and was crying and Mary had thumped
Ben because he'd stood on her foot.

Miss Merryman had to scream to get
everyone to stand still and be quiet so she
could unlock the door.

Everyone charged to their desks,
although she'd asked us all to go
quietly and not to push.

There was a kind of disappointed groan
in the room. Then silence. I think
we'd all hoped to find another blob. But
there was nothing, no more blobs or
blotches on anyone's books.

Chapter Three

The next morning there was another big rush when we came into class. Everyone was still half hoping to find something on one of their books. We were all quite jealous of Graham and Emma. The blobs had singled them out in some way. But as the day wore on and nothing else happened we all began to forget about them. Miss Merryman still locked the door though, at break and lunch-time.

It was after second break I found it. It was there on my desk, right in the middle of my English book. A large rusty red blob, shiny like the others and quite dry. I'm not sure what I felt. Excited and special, as though I too had been chosen.

Everyone crowded round, patting me on the back. Miss Merryman came over to my desk.

Then Barry Edwards shouted,

It must have been something about the way she said it, very slowly and seriously: "But how? How can they possibly have got there? All the doors and windows were locked."

I'm sure she didn't mean to frighten us, but we all suddenly went very quiet. I heard someone say, "It's really spooky. I don't like it."

Someone even began crying.

Miss Merryman tried to calm everyone down again with things like,

There must be a simple explanation, it's absolutely nothing to worry about.

"But Miss, if the doors and windows are all locked, where can it have come from?"

Barry Edwards pointed to the ceiling. "Perhaps it came from up there."
"I said there was a body there," wailed Tom Dent.

Everyone looked up. But we couldn't see any marks or drips on the ceiling.
"I'm sure it hasn't come from there," said Miss Merryman, "that's Class 5 isn't it?"

"No, Miss," said Barry, "Class 5 is one more floor up. There's just an empty classroom above us. It's always locked."
"It hasn't been used for years and years and years," said Louise.
"It has, it has," Sarah Smith blurted out. "I heard something up there yesterday when I had to stay in at play. Footsteps and something being dragged across the floor. I'm sure of it."

Oh shut up!

screamed Ben.

"Now just to reassure you," said Miss Merryman, "why don't we all go and look. We can be detectives," she said in a very bright, jolly way. "I want you to sit here as quiet as mice, while I go and get the key from Mr Brown."

Charlie, who'd been very quiet up to now, put up his hand. "Someone died up there once Miss, a long, long time ago."

"Honest, Miss, my older brother told me.
There was once a fire at the school, more
than a hundred years ago. A little girl
died. That classroom's meant to be
haunted. Some of the fifth year found out
about it from a newspaper at the library,
when they were doing a project for the
school's hundredth anniversary."

"I don't want to stay here. It's too
spooky," wailed Emma.
"Now don't be silly," said Miss
Merryman. "There's nothing to be
worried about. I shall only be gone a
minute, just stay quietly in your seats."
But Miss Merryman seemed to be gone
for ages. We all sat in silence, until Barry
began to make ghost noises from the back
of the class. Some people in the front
screamed. Then we all started laughing
and felt a
lot better.

At last Miss Merryman came back with
Mr Brown. Mr Brown did not look at all
pleased about the noise and he seemed
rather annoyed with Miss Merryman. I
felt sorry for Miss Merryman, she was
trying her best.

Mr Brown walked round the class.

He looked at
the blobs on the
exercise books.

He looked at the
creative writing
on the walls.

He looked at us.

I hope you are not giving Miss Merryman any trouble?

NO sir.

We all shook our heads.

Miss Merryman interrupted. "I thought it would be helpful if we all visited the empty classroom upstairs. The children seem a little worried about these blobs. I'm sure there's a simple explanation. We could turn this into a sort of project."

"If you think it would be helpful, Miss Merryman," said Mr Brown.

But please return the key to me when you have finished. And I don't want to see any children charging around the school

Miss Merryman turned to us with her finger on her lips. "I want you to follow me, children, as quietly as you can."

We all filed out of class past Mr Brown. Of course Barry Edwards snorted by mistake and a few people giggled, but with a lot of 'sh's' from everybody there was quiet again.

We tiptoed after Miss Merryman, along the corridor and up the stairs. We could feel Mr Brown watching us, but we didn't turn round.

I was at the end of the line. I felt he was staring right through me. There was something odd about him. I don't know what it was. He just didn't seem to be like a real teacher. For a start he was a lot stricter than teachers usually are, and not at all friendly. He was more like one of those teachers you see on old films.

Miss Bell was usually busy in her office when she wasn't taking a class, but he was always wandering about the place.

I began to remember all the strange things I'd noticed about him. Like him bending down by the grass under our classroom window as though he'd lost something. The way he walked round and round the long grass at the edge of the playground, just staring at the ground.

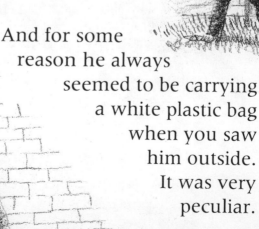

And for some reason he always seemed to be carrying a white plastic bag when you saw him outside. It was very peculiar.

When we reached the top of the stairs, I turned round to see if he was still watching. He'd disappeared.

We all crowded round the door of the empty classroom.

There will be absolutely nothing in there but old tables and chairs.

There'll be a ghost in there.

What if the murderer still there?-

I bet there'll be a body.

"Mr Brown says it's just used as a store-room now," said Miss Merryman very firmly.

She put the key in the lock and tried to turn it. It wouldn't move. She tried again.
"Let me try," said Graham.
"It's no use," said Miss Merryman. "It doesn't fit. Mr Brown must have given us the wrong key."
She passed the key to Graham. "Will you and Jack take the key back to Mr Brown and ask him for another one?" she said.

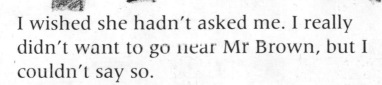

I wished she hadn't asked me. I really didn't want to go near Mr Brown, but I couldn't say so.

Graham knocked on Mr Brown's door. There was no answer. He tried again. We heard a loud voice.
"Just a moment."

We had to wait quite a long time, then we heard his voice again.
"Enter."

We slowly opened the door and went in.
Mr Brown was sitting behind Miss Bell's
desk.
"Yes. What do you want?"
"Please, Sir, Miss Merryman
thinks you've given us
the wrong key,"
said Graham.

Can we have another one?

"I think he's lying," I said to Graham as we walked back. "I think he's got the right key, but he doesn't want us to go into that room."

"What are you talking about?" said Graham.

"I think Mr Brown's got something in that room and he doesn't want us to see it. I'm sure of it."

"You're as bad as the others," said Graham, "with ghosts and bodies."

"It's nothing to do with the blobs or ghosts or anything. I just feel strange about him. He's odd. He's up to something."

"Perhaps there really is a body up there," laughed Graham, "perhaps he's murdered Miss Bell!"

I felt a shiver run through me.

Don't. Graham dont joke. I know something isn't right. I just know it.

Headmaster

We all went back to the classroom. Miss Merryman tried to be extra jolly and kind. We didn't talk about blobs or ghosts or being detectives any more. We began a new geography project. I couldn't really concentrate on anything. I managed to pass a note to Graham. I wanted to come back after school, but not on my own. I felt sure Graham would help me.

Chapter Four

Graham and I lived quite near the school. We often went that way after school to play on our bikes in the park. We had to be back home by 5.30 for tea.

I got there before Graham. I looked over the wall. You could get a good view of the playground and car park from the road without being seen. There was no-one about at all. All the cars had gone, except one – the one Mr Brown had come in that morning.

Graham sped up on his bike. I held up my finger for him to be quiet. He crept along the wall beside me.

We waited there a long time. We thought
we could see a figure in one of the
windows. First in our class, then the room
above, the empty room. We were too far
away to see who it was for certain, but I
knew it was him.

We crept through the school gates. There were some shrubs near the car park. We could hide in there and get a better view. There was one open bit you had to run across to reach the shrubs.

Graham went first. I followed. I was sure I would be seen. I ran as fast as I could. I just made it, but my heart was beating.

Then the main door opened slowly. It was
Mr Brown. Perhaps he had seen me. He
seemed to be coming towards us. Then he
turned right and walked towards the grass
under our classroom window. He was
carrying something in his right hand. We
could see it clearly from our side. It was a
knife! Not a penknife or dinner knife.
It had a long, shiny, curved blade.

I gasped. I heard Graham give a kind of gulp. Mr Brown stopped for a moment and turned towards us. We froze. We didn't move or breathe.

Then he carried on walking. We saw him bend down under the classroom window. He had his back to us. We couldn't make out what he was doing. He seemed to be moving his arm up and down as though he was wiping the knife on the grass. Then he got a bag out of his pocket and put something in it. He stood up at last and walked back into school.

I don't know how long we hid there. We
didn't dare move or speak. It had started
to get dark. Neither of us wanted to move
until he'd gone. We just wanted him to
get into his car and drive far away and
never come back. At last the school door
opened again.

Mr Brown came out, carrying a huge
cardboard box. It looked very heavy. He
stood for a moment looking around, then
walked slowly towards his car.

He somehow got it on to the back seat.
Then, leaving the door open, he turned
and went back inside the school. What
was in the box? Was it Miss Bell, or part
of Miss Bell? It was too terrible to think
about. It was like a horrible dream.
"We've got to see what's in the box,"
whispered Graham.

I followed Graham in a daze. I was so
scared I didn't know what I was doing.
We'd just reached the car when Mr
Brown came out again.

I screamed.

It was Graham who saved us.
"We were just passing, Mr Brown," he
gulped.
"Can we give you a hand?"
"Thank you, no," said Mr Brown.
"You children should be at home now,
you'd better get off."

We ran to our bikes and rode home very,
very quickly.

Chapter Five

I couldn't sleep that night. My head was spinning. I couldn't make sense of it all. The blobs. Mr Brown. They had to be connected. But how?

I was too frightened to close my eyes.
Every time I did, I seemed to see
Mr Brown up there in that room. He
had Miss Bell with him and there was a
knife in his hand. I saw the boxes and
Mr Brown's hand raised above his head.
And then I saw the little girl, the ghost
with her white dress and long hair.
She seemed to be trying to stop him.
There was blood on the floor . . . .

Suddenly it all began to fit together and make sense. The girl had come back to warn us. The blobs were a warning. A warning of something terrible that was going to happen, or had happened, or would still happen.

Who would be next after Miss Bell? I couldn't bear to think about it. I couldn't even close my eyes in case I saw him. I stayed awake most of the night, tossing and turning. I had to stop anything else happening. I would tell Miss Merryman. She would listen. She would do something.

In the morning, I didn't want to go to
school. I felt terrible. But I didn't have a
temperature, so I had to go.

At least there were no more blobs on
anyone's books. But I was late and
Miss Merryman was already doing
the register when I got there. There was
no time to speak to her before we had
to go into assembly.

I hung at the back with Graham. I felt
very shaky. I didn't want to see
Mr Brown again, not after . . . what he'd
done to Miss Bell.

I didn't even look up until Graham
nudged me. I couldn't believe it. There on
the stage, on the table next to Mr Brown,
was another huge cardboard box. I felt
horribly sick. I could hardly hear what he
was saying. Was it something about
Miss Bell? Was he telling us why
Miss Bell wasn't coming back anymore?

I thought I would faint. Graham nudged
me again.
"She's coming back tomorrow."
"What?"
"Miss Bell. Listen. He's saying, she's
coming back tomorrow."

I listened.
". . . so as I was saying, I'm sure you will
all be pleased to hear that Miss Bell will
be well enough to return to school
tomorrow."

Mr Brown pointed to the box.
"Now I expect you must all be wondering what is inside this large cardboard box. It is a small present from me to the school."

I watched in disbelief as Mr Brown slowly took out the long curved knife from his briefcase.

With two swift strokes he slit the front
sides of the box, revealing a large wooden
rabbit hutch.

Everyone clapped.

"Miss Bell kindly gave me permission to
use the old classroom in the evenings to
make my daughter's birthday surprise. So
I decided I would make one for the school
as well."
Mr Brown lifted his hand for quiet.

"I have very much enjoyed my short stay
with you. I may see some of you again
from time to time.

Miss Bell has kindly said I may come back to collect the excellent dandelions which grow around your playing field. My daughter's rabbit has grown very fond of them."

I was still staring at the rabbit hutch when Graham gave me a push. Everyone was filing out of the hall.

"Huh, rabbits!" said Graham.

So much for dead bodies.

Miss Merryman hadn't been in assembly.
When we got back into class, she was
standing by Barry Edwards' desk. She
was holding a small bottle of red liquid.
Barry blushed.

Sorry miss. It was just a joke. The first blobs gave me the idea. It was me that did Jack's book and mine yesterday. It's Dracula's blood you know, pretend blood you paint on. You get it from joke shops. It was easy to dab a bit on without being seen on my way out to play.

"What do you mean, just Jack's book and your own? Please sit down Barry. It's not very funny. I'm pleased you've owned up, but I'd be much happier if you'd told me the whole truth."

"But honestly, Miss, I only did the last
two books."
"Well I'm afraid you'll have to bring in
some pocket money to pay for them. I'll
return the liquid at the end of the day.
Please take it home and keep it there."
"Yes Miss, thank you Miss," said Barry.

I thought she was really going to tell him
off. I know she didn't believe him. But
she just told him to get on with his work.

It was Miss Merryman's last day, too.
We were going to miss her. We'd really
enjoyed the creative writing lesson. Barry
wrote a big 'Goodbye' on the blackboard
during last break.

Miss Merryman smiled.
"Thank you everyone. Perhaps I'll see
you again some time. By the way,
Mr Brown gave me the right key today.
There really are only old desks and tables
up there, I thought I'd better check!"

Chapter Six

The next day Mrs North was back and so were some of the others. But Barry Edwards had got flu and was away, and Sarah Smith was off too.

It was a terrible morning. The rain was pouring down. Graham and I were soaked by the time we got to school. The sky was very dark. We managed to get in before the very worst of it. By the time we were all in class, the rain was really belting down, bouncing off the concrete in the playground and beating against the windows.

We were glad to be inside and it was nice to see Mrs North again. And then the thunder started. It was so loud we hardly heard the scream. We knew something was wrong by the way Mary was jumping up and down and waving her arms.

I've got one
I've got one

My heart was racing. She couldn't have got one. It was over. It was all over. It had been nothing, just Barry Edwards . . . but as Mary held up her book, we saw it, all of us. There, right in the middle of her book, red and shiny and about four centimetres across was another blob. And this one was still wet . . .